MR. MISCHIEF

by Roger Hargreaves

PSS!
PRICE STERN SLOAN

Poor Mr. Happy had had a tiring day.

Rushing here and there and back again cheering people up was hard work.

"Phew," he sighed, as he went into his house and sat down for a well-earned rest on a kitchen chair.

But then, do you know what happened?

It fell to bits!

BUMP, went poor Mr. Happy.

"That's all I need," he said. "I rather think that I have had a visit from Mr. Mischief."

He was right!

Outside Mr. Happy's house, and running away as fast as his little legs would carry him, was a small mischievous figure.

Mr. Mischief!

"Oh mischief, glorious mischief," he cried. "I do so love it!"

And he ran, giggling, into the night.

The next morning there was a knock at Mr. Greedy's front door, but when he went to answer it, there was no one there.

What was there was a box.

And inside the box was a large chocolate cake filled with cream and with the most delicious-looking pink icing.

Mr. Greedy's eyes gleamed.

He licked his lips, and shut his eyes, and opened his mouth, and took a large bite.

UGH!

The chocolate wasn't chocolate.

It was mud!

The cream inside wasn't cream.

It was cotton!!

And that delicious-looking pink icing wasn't icing at all.

It was toothpaste!!!

That's not all.

That very same morning, Mr. Funny discovered that someone had filled his hat with molasses.

Very sticky molasses!

Can you guess who that someone might have been?

However, that very same afternoon, Mr. Mischief did something that he would regret.

He was walking along through the woods, looking for mischief, when he came across a wizard.

A fast-asleep wizard.

"I know," giggled Mr. Mischief, "I'll change the wizard's wand for an ordinary piece of wood and then he can't do any magic.

He grinned a mischievous grin, and crept quietly towards the slumbering wizard.

Mr. Mischief reached carefully out and seized the wizard's magic wand.

But what he didn't know was that wizards' wands don't like to be seized.

"HELP!" shrieked the wand in a high, shrill voice, and awakened the wizard, who in turn seized Mr. Mischief by his nose.

Which was extremely painful!

"Led go ob by node!" cried Mr. Mischief.

"I know who you are," said the wizard. "You're that Mr. Mischief who sawed through poor Mr. Happy's chair legs, and," he continued, "baked a rather unusual cake for poor Mr. Greedy, and," he went on, "put molasses in poor Mr. Funny's hat! I've been hearing all about you," he added.

"Led go ob by node," cried Mr. Mischief again.

"Very well," said the wizard. "But don't believe that you can get away with being as mischievous as that!"

And, as he let go of Mr. Mischief's nose, he got hold of his magic wand, and waved it.

"Beware," he said, and went off.

"Silly wizard," muttered Mr. Mischief. "Can't you take a joke?"

And he went home.

"Silly wizard," he said again, as he sat down in his kitchen.

BUMP!

"Silly, silly, silly, wizard," groaned Mr. Mischief, picking himself up. "Him and his silly magic!"

And he made himself some porridge for supper.

"Mmmm," smiled Mr. Mischief, as he put a large spoonful of poridge into his mouth.

"AARGH!"

Somehow, as if by magic (which of course it was), the porridge had turned into . . . sawdust!

"Oh dear," spluttered Mr. Mischief. "Perhaps I had better not get up to quite so much mischief in the future after all."

And he went upstairs.

He jumped into bed.

SPLOSH!

The bed was full of raspberry jam.

Ugh!

"Oh dear, oh dear," sighed Mr. Mischief. "I think I definitely must not get up to quite so much mischief in the future!"

And do you know something?

The day after he was as good as gold.

And the next day.

And the day after that.

It lasted a week!

And then, that old mischievous urge got the better of him.

He just couldn't help himself.

It was a Saturday night.

He crept into Mr. Fussy's house when he was fast asleep, and can you guess what he did?

"Oh, what a beautiful piece of perfect mischief," he cried, as he ran giggling home.

He'd cut off half Mr. Fussy's moustache!!

Isn't that terrible?

Poor, poor Mr. Fussy.

He was absolutely horrified when he awoke and found out.

But even that terrible piece of mischief is not the end of Mr. Mischief's story.

So . . .

. . . before you read this last page, just take a look out of the window.

Go on!

You can't see a small mischievous figure anywhere about.

Can you?

Are you sure?